LADYBIRD BOOKS, INC.
Auburn, Maine 04210 U.S.A.
© LADYBIRD BOOKS LTD 1989
Loughborough, Leicestershire, England

Printed in England

The Easter Bunny's Helpers

By Michaela Muntean

Illustrated by Deborah Colvin Borgo

Ladybird Books

It was the day before Easter, and everything was ready
in Bunny Hollow. The speckled eggs had just the right amount
of speckles. The striped eggs were perfectly striped.
And there were hundreds of other eggs, dyed in every color
of the rainbow.

Everything was ready
for Easter morning.

Everything, that is, except the
Easter Bunny himself.

He was in bed with an earache, and, as you can imagine,
that can be a very serious thing for a bunny.

The Easter Bunny's nieces and nephews tried to make him feel better. Benny brought him an ice pack. Denny brought him a hot-water bottle. Jenny brought him some carrot juice. And Penny read to him from his favorite book.

But nothing seemed to help.

"My ears hurt so much that I can't even hop properly," groaned the Easter Bunny, and back to bed he went.

"I know I'll be fine in a day or two," the Easter Bunny told his nieces and nephews. "But Easter is tomorrow. I just won't be able to deliver the children's Easter eggs this year. One of you will have to go instead."

"I'll go!" said Benny, Denny, Jenny, and Penny all at once.

The Easter Bunny smiled. "Thank you all for offering to help," he said. "I will have to send Benny, because he is the biggest and strongest. It is a long way to hop, and there are many eggs to deliver."

The Easter Bunny showed
Benny a special map, which only he and
Santa Claus had. "This is a shortcut around
the world," he explained. "You will need it in
order to deliver all the Easter eggs by morning."

Benny studied the map for a long time.
At last he was ready. Feeling proud
and excited, he waved good-by
to everyone in Bunny Hollow,
and set off.

Benny had never been away from home before. He had never even seen any other animals, except for other bunnies! So he was very surprised when he met a small animal with a long bushy tail.

"What kind of bunny are you?" Benny asked.

The little animal laughed. "I'm not a bunny," he said. "I'm a squirrel, and I live in that oak tree."

"How do you get up there?" Benny asked. "Can you hop that high?"

"Of course not!" the squirrel said. "I climb up—like this." And he scampered up the tree and down again, faster than Benny could say "hippity-hop."

Benny set down the basket of Easter eggs. "I wish *I* could do that," he said.

"And whoooo are you?" said a voice.

Benny looked around. "Did you say that?" he asked the squirrel.

"That's the hoot owl," the squirrel explained. "She lives in this tree, too."

The hoot owl swooped down to get
a closer look at Benny. On the way, she woke
up a robin, who also flew down from her nest.

"Whoooo are you?" the hoot owl asked again.

"I'm Benny," said Benny. Then he told them about Easter, and his uncle, and his uncle's earache. "And these," he said proudly, "are the Easter eggs I am going to deliver."

By now a deer, a duck, and
a frog had joined the group.
They all gathered around
to look at the eggs.

"Those eggs are lovely," chirped the robin. "Now come up and see *my* eggs!"

"And come and meet my ducklings," said the duck.

"And my tadpole," added the frog.

"Then you must stay for dinner," said the deer. "We'll make our special nut-berry stew."

Benny didn't know what to say.
He wanted to stay with his new friends,
but he had an important job to do,
and it was getting late.

"I will stay for a little while," he said.
"Then I must be on my way."

First Benny visited the robin's nest.

"I will have to tell my uncle about this beautiful shade of blue," he said when he saw the robin's eggs.

Next he followed the duck and the frog to the pond, where he splashed and played with the ducklings and the tadpole.

"I can't wait to tell my brother and sisters about this!" he said.

"Dinner's ready," called the deer, and they all sat down around the fire.

"This stew is delicious," said Benny. "I will make some for everyone in Bunny Hollow when I get home."

Benny was having such a good time that the "little while" turned into a very long while. He was just leaning back against the oak tree, when he suddenly bumped into the basket of eggs.

"Oh, no!" he cried, jumping up. "I forgot all about Easter!"

Benny tried not to cry when he realized how careless he had been. "I'll never get these eggs to the children by morning!" he moaned.

"You know," said the deer, "I can run very fast. Maybe I could help deliver some of them."

"We could help, too," said the owl, the duck, and the robin. "We'll fly as fast as we can."

"Frog and I will help, too," said the squirrel.

"Do you think we could do it in time?" asked Benny.

"We can try," they said.

And off they went, running, flying, scampering, and hopping as fast as they could.

And so, that year, for the first
time ever, there was
an Easter Deer...

an Easter Duck...

an Easter Robin...

an Easter Owl...

an Easter Frog...

an Easter Squirrel, and...

an Easter Benny, who delivered all the
rainbow-colored eggs in time for Easter morning.